Careers For
Artistic Types

Interviews by Andrew Kaplan

Photographs by Eddie Keating and Carrie Boretz

CHOICES
The Millbrook Press
Brookfield, Connecticut

Produced in association with Agincourt Press.

Photographs by Eddie Keating, except: Mercy Van Vlack (Carrie Boretz), Schecter Lee (Carrie Boretz), Wynn Herou Gubrud (Mark Bertram), Rick Alley (Steve Jones), John Karl (Carrie Boretz), Elizabeth Bailey (Kathy Fairfield), Kevin Coyle (Carrie Boretz).

Cataloging-in-Publication Data

Kaplan, Andrew.
Careers for artistic types/interviews by Andrew Kaplan, photographs by Eddie Keating and Carrie Boretz.

64 p.; ill.: (Choices)
Bibliography: p.
Includes index.

Summary: Interviews with fourteen people who work in careers of interest to young people who like art.
1. Art – Vocational guidance. (Art – Study and teaching).
I. Keating, Eddie, ill.   II. Boretz, Carrie, ill.
III. Title.   IV. Series.
N 8350 K141   1991   702.3 KAP
ISBN 1-878841-20-3
ISBN 1-878841-46-7 (pbk.)
Photographs copyright in the names of the photographers.

Contents

Introduction

In this book, 14 people who work in art-related fields talk about their careers — what their work involves, how they got started, and what they like (and dislike) about it. They tell you things you should know before beginning an art-related career, and show you how a love of art and design can lead to many different types of jobs.

Some are jobs in such traditional art fields as sculpture, graphic design, and photography. Others bring artistic flair to the fields of interior design and fashion design. And some employ art skills in even more unusual ways — in toy design and comic book publishing, for example. Finally, some don't use classic art skills at all, because you don't have to draw or paint or sculpt to have a career that's related to art. You can be creative as a make-up artist or a food stylist. And if you just like being around art, you may want to be an art librarian.

The 14 careers described here are just the beginning, so don't limit your sights. At the end of this book, you'll find short descriptions of 13 more careers you may want to explore, as well as suggestions on how to get more information. Art is everywhere in the business world. If you're an artistic type, you'll find a wide range of career choices open to you.

Joan B. Storey, M.S.W., M.B.A.
Series Career Consultant

"It's great when you bring a new idea to a client and they love it."

JIM HYBISKE

TOY DESIGNER

San Francisco, California

WHAT I DO:

I'm a partner in a firm that specializes in design work for the toy industry. We develop products, packaging, and brochures. Since we have a knowledge of the toy industry, toy manufacturers come to us, rather than to a general design firm.

Toy manufacturers develop most of their products themselves. However, they assign some product development to firms like ours. These assignments take different forms. Sometimes they're open-ended — the company says, "Bring us an outdoor game." Other times we're asked to do a specific task, such as designing a baby rattle that has certain features and meets certain requirements.

Regardless of the assignment, we always begin with a client meeting. Then we sketch a variety of concepts and have a second meeting at which the sketches get narrowed down. Often the good features of one idea get combined with the best features of another. Eventually we come up with a final design from which we build a model.

Sometimes, though, we come up with an idea on our own, and try to sell it to a company. Again, the process starts with sketches. And then if a company shows interest, we build a prototype, or working model. Finally, the toy company's marketing people have to make a decision. If they want to go ahead, we figure out logistics — engineering, materials, manufacturing, and costs. Usually the company takes over around this time. It's rare that we're involved in the production process.

Jim works on a model of a dinosaur-shaped package.

Jim's company specializes in catalogues like this one.

Although product development is interesting, most of what we do is packaging and catalogue work. It's not really toy design, but you have to understand toys in order to do it properly. We've designed packages in the shapes of dinosaurs, jeeps, and biplanes. We've even designed a package in the shape of a rhinoceros.

HOW I GOT STARTED:

I stumbled into this work. Originally, I got a degree in industrial design, which is concerned with mechanics, materials, and how people work with objects. My first job was for Mattel, the big toy company. After a while,

though, I wanted to get out of the toy industry, so I got a job with a design group in a glass company.

But once I was out of toys, I found that I missed them. So I went to work for a Japanese toy company where I did everything — product development, catalogues, packaging, and instructions. Eventually my partner and I founded our own company.

HOW I FEEL ABOUT IT:

Obviously, the creative aspect of the work is important. Part of my talent is being able to draw, sketch, and visualize ideas, and this job gives me a lot of opportunity to do that. It's great when you bring a new idea to a client and he loves it. I also like seeing a product when it's in the stores.

The biggest problem is the incessant deadlines. They're always tight, and the work seems to come all at once. Depending on the deadlines, our hours can be pretty long. At a large toy company, in contrast, the work is basically 9-to-5.

Aside from the uneven workload, running your own business has its own advantages and disadvantages, much like freelancing. We don't have security, benefits, or insurance. On the other hand, we're the masters of our own destiny. If a client is difficult, we can decide not to work with him. In a corporation, you can be stuck working with tough people for many years.

WHAT YOU SHOULD KNOW: People have misconceptions about this work. They say, "Isn't that fun? You draw toys all day." But it's a brutal, fast business, and it's relatively low-paying. If you develop your own concept, and it's a hit toy, you can earn a lot of money. But when you do work for other people, it's on an hourly basis, and you don't do as well as lawyers or engineers, who also work by the hour.

To do this job well, it helps to know both graphic and industrial design. You must be able to visualize ideas and sketch them. But it's also good to understand materials and production. You need to be able to answer questions like "What should it be made out of?" and "How can I make it?"

Jim combines creativity and technical skills.

"As a child, I was always painting, drawing, making things."

JENNY KRASNER

SCULPTOR

Ridgefield, New Jersey

WHAT I DO:
I'm a sculptor. That may sound like just molding clay or chipping away at stone, but to make my pieces I do just about everything. I weld, I paint, I plaster, and so on.

For the past seven months, I've been working on a series of large sculptures. Each one shows a person in an architectural space — a room, a doorway, or whatever. Actually, the spaces are almost like stages for the figures.

To make the frames for the spaces, I use thin steel rods. I bend them and bolt them together to suggest the outline of a person in a space. Then I use shorter rods to fill in some of the sculpture's details, such as the person's ribs. Finally, I take whatever I have lying around, such as bits of wood or canvas, and I use string to tie these bits and pieces to the frame. The result is my sculpture. Obviously, it's not strictly realistic, but I think it captures the feeling of a person in a place.

HOW I GOT STARTED:
I've always been interested in art. It was inevitable, I guess. My father was an art dealer. My mother was a painter. If my parents had been dentists, I'd probably be a dentist.

As a child, I was always painting, drawing, making things. That never stopped. But when I got out of high school, I didn't go straight to art school. I knew my work would be stronger if I learned about everything else first — literature, history, and science, rather than just art. I knew a good, well-rounded education would help me see and show things in a broader and more interesting way.

So I went to Hamilton

Jenny welds thin steel rods for a new sculpture.

11

College, and got a liberal arts degree. Then I went to Oxford University in England to study fine arts.

After Oxford, I didn't know what to do. Although I wanted to continue my art, I didn't believe that I could make a living at it. I think we're taught from an early age that if you really like something, you'll never be able to make it your life's work. So for about a year, I just did temporary jobs to get by.

I took an advertising course because I thought it

Jenny's work is often physically demanding.

might be a creative field. I even worked as an assistant at the Museum of Modern Art in New York. But nothing felt right. One day, though, I got a commission to do a large outdoor mobile, and I suddenly realized I could do this for a living. Ever since then, I've been working only on my art.

HOW I FEEL ABOUT IT: The main reason I'm doing this is that I don't get total satisfaction from doing anything else. Let me try to explain: Suppose you build a bookcase for your stereo. Doing a practical thing well — that gives you satisfaction. But that's only a fraction of the satisfaction I get from completing a piece of art that I think is good.

Of course, being an artist can also be quite difficult. Recently I spent two months sending out slides of my larger sculptures. When no one was interested, I told myself that it was only because I hadn't been around long enough. I reminded myself that only people with lots of room and lots of money — millionaires and museums — buy this kind of work. Since then, I've gotten commissions for smaller pieces, but my experience with large sculptures can still upset me.

Jenny uses all sorts of scrap material in her work.

WHAT YOU SHOULD KNOW:
The way movies show artists is all wrong. Movie artists are crazy people who work all night and only when they feel like it. But I think art is a day thing. It's got to be done when you have all your energy. It's a 9-to-5 job and if you don't do it every day, you don't get paid.

You need more than just art skills to be an artist. You need to be a business person — orderly, professional, and patient. Slides of your work must be sent out regularly. You must dress well and not look strange. You have to try to answer questions, even if you think they're stupid. And whatever happens, you can't get mad when people don't like your work.

You also have to be flexible and be able to make sacrifices. Most artists work at other jobs to support themselves. I'm lucky. I'm living off my art.

"What looks great to one person may look terrible to another."

STEVE AARON

GRAPHIC DESIGNER

Stamford, Connecticut

WHAT I DO:
I design promotional materials, sales materials, and packaging. The promotional materials and packaging are what most people see. For example, when you open your Sunday newspaper, a page of coupons usually falls out. This is called an FSI, which is short for Free-Standing Insert. I design a lot of these. I also design the actual packages that products come in, and sometimes I design sales kits. These are arrangements of sales materials, such as brochures and displays, that a sales force uses to help sell its company's products.

Because I work at a studio with other designers, most of our projects begin with several designers producing rough sketches of different designs. Then, after our art director has reviewed the sketches, we tighten up the good ideas and produce a second set of sketches that are more detailed. Then we do paste-ups, using actual printed type and clearer pictures. And finally, we show these layouts to the client. After they've been revised and approved, we do a color layout, which includes all the photos and illustrations.

HOW I GOT STARTED:
Originally I was interested in cartooning, which led me to college at the School of Visual Arts in New York City. However, as I took classes, my focus began to change. For a while I thought about concentrating on painting. But I realized that I had to support myself, so I kept looking for another route.

My interest in packaging and promotional design developed in my second year at S.V.A. I had a design class

Steve discusses the color options for a new design.

15

in which I was asked to redesign the packaging of the Baby Ruth candy bar. My effort wasn't very good, but I realized then that I loved three-dimensional design. The next year, I took a packaging class and decided that package design was the route I would take. I rounded out my schooling with an independent study in package design my senior year.

While I was at S.V.A. I built up a portfolio of my work. I also built up my business contacts. The portfolio and the contacts helped me get some freelance work. Then I got this staff job.

HOW I FEEL ABOUT IT:

One of the things I like best about this job is the variety of work that comes in. I get to work on all kinds of things. One day, I may design a brochure for a line of perfumes. The next day, it might be a marketing handbook for blue jeans. I need that variety. It keeps the work challenging and exciting.

Another challenging aspect to this job is that it's all based on opinions. What looks great to one person may look terrible to another. Your art director may like a concept, but the client might hate it. Sometimes the client will even okay an idea and tell you to finalize it. But in the meantime, the client's market research department tests your idea on groups of potential customers and decides that it won't work. So, just when you think you're ready to go, you've got to start all over again. The

Steve's job involves working closely with many people.

Steve looks over some art with another designer.

process can be very long, but you've got to stick with it.

WHAT YOU SHOULD KNOW:
This job involves long hours. When you're trying to beat deadlines, it's not quitting time until you're finished. Often your lunch will be quick, or late, or both. To do this job, you have to be able to work and thrive under the pressure — if you don't enjoy pressure, then you shouldn't do this. You also have to know how to pace yourself. You have to know when and how to ease up, or you'll burn out.

You also need to be creative, patient, and able to handle criticism. The creativity and patience are neces-sary for the endless revisions of ideas. As for the criticism — well, art directors and clients will rip you apart. You've got to be able to listen to them, to take it.

To get into this work, you have to go to a good art school and make good con-tacts. You can do okay paywise in a staff job, but if you really want to make more, the next step is to be-come a creative director and run things. Freelancers in high demand also make good livings.

Another thing you should do is learn to work with com-puters, particularly the Macintosh. More and more studios are becoming com-pletely computerized.

"Too few comic books are heroic or interesting."

MERCY VAN VLACK

COMIC BOOK PUBLISHER

New York, New York

WHAT I DO:

My partner and I publish comic books. I do some of the actual drawing myself, and I interview the artists who do the rest of it. My partner Ken works with the writers. After the comics are written and drawn, I get them ready to go to the printer.

The art that you see in comics is the result of a process that breaks down into several steps. First you draw the outlines of the figures in pencil. Next you do the inking, using a brush or a pen to make the lines, backgrounds, and shadings that give comics life. Finally you do the lettering and, if your comic is in color, the coloring. Our comics are in black-and-white, so we don't do that last step.

Mercy prepares artwork. In addition to publishing the books, she does some of the drawing.

HOW I GOT STARTED:

My first art skills came from imitating the styles of the comic books I read. When I was in high school, I would finish my tests as fast as I could so I could draw pictures on the back of them. This got me into trouble sometimes, because my teachers felt I wasn't spending enough time on the front of the tests. But lots of times my drawings helped my grades. For English class, I drew pictures of Shakespearean characters and their stage costumes. For science, I drew things like cross-sections of shellfish. This earned me lots of extra credit.

After high school I went to a two-year school where I learned the technical skills that all artists need. At first, I used these skills in a series of jobs that were not related to comic books. I did artwork and layouts for a newspaper.

I also worked for the Yellow Pages and an ad agency.

But while I was going to school, and doing these jobs, I kept drawing comics. I also started selling my work to fanzines. Fanzines are low-budget magazines about comics that are written and illustrated by fans and collectors. They don't pay much — only a few dollars for paper and postage — but fanzines are a good way for comic-book artists to get their start. They're how I got mine.

HOW I FEEL ABOUT IT:

My partner and I take a lot of pride in our comic books.

We started publishing them in order to fill a void left by the death of a great writer and friend named E. Nelson Bridwell. He wrote Superman, and a lot of other genuine comic-book heroes. Nelson's characters cared about people, and his comics were educational in that they were based on legends from other cultures.

After Nelson died, Ken and I realized that too few comic books were heroic or interesting — most just showed lots of killing for no reason. So we decided to publish comics like Nelson's — comics with heroic heroes and real cultural details based on myths and legends.

WHAT YOU SHOULD KNOW:

If you want to enter this field, the best advice I can give you is practice, practice, practice. Send your pictures to fanzines. Join a writing group. Take drawing classes. Keep showing your work to people and publishers. Study a wide range of art and literature for ideas.

When you send out work, look for publishers who use your style. For instance, if your art is realistic, send it to a place that uses realistic art. And if you're going to be

Good comic book illustrators can make $40,000 a year.

Mercy and Ken publish comics with genuine heroes.

an assistant, find an artist who's already doing the kind of art you like. In big companies, there's usually a "bullpen," a department where corrections to artwork are done in-house, and you may be able to find work there.

There's a wide range of pay for comic book illustrators. It depends on the task — whether you're penciling, inking, lettering, or coloring — and your speed. People will pay you well if you're very fast or very, very good. Illustrators can make $40,000 per year and, in a few cases, as much as $100,000.

Many people use their comic-book skills to earn livings in other fields. For example, directors who shoot movies and television all use storyboards, which are sketches that show the action to be filmed. If you're fast, you can make money drawing those. Comic-book artists have also gotten work drawing illustrations for training manuals. Basically, whenever drawings are needed, comic-book skills are useful.

"The most important traits to have are tenacity and persistence."

SCHECTER LEE

COMMERCIAL PHOTOGRAPHER

New York, New York

WHAT I DO:

I take pictures for a living. Working out of my own studio, I do portraits, catalogue photographs, and advertising work. Some of my work comes through word-of-mouth, because I've been in the business a long time. Other jobs I pursue, or interview for.

People think all there is to my job is a snap of the shutter, that fraction of a second, but they're wrong. Most of my work is done off-camera. First I get an understanding of my subject. Then I create the best setting for it. This includes lighting and styling. Lighting involves the use of both light and shadows, shadows that can help bring out character. Styling is the mix of objects and colors in a shot. These elements create the mood. Mood is very important. It's what you remember.

Schecter takes care to create the best setting.

Then, in addition to the actual photography, there's the business aspect of my work. Paperwork, returning phone calls, finding work — all of this is very important. In fact, it's almost more important than the photography itself. Studio photography is very expensive. Equipment, even in a one-man studio like mine, can run to $75,000 or $100,000. So you've got to keep up with the business end, or else you'll go under. You've got to take it very seriously.

HOW I GOT STARTED:

I got into photography by chance. I studied literature in college. Then I moved to New York and tried to write. Writing was what I wanted to do then. But after a while I turned 30 and I still wasn't going anywhere. In fact, I was living in a seedy hotel, and things were miserable. Then, by chance, I got a

Schecter carefully examines contact sheets.

temporary job at the Metropolitan Museum of Art.

There I met and became an apprentice to a famous photographer named Lee Bolton. Together we photographed a well-known collection of primitive art. It was difficult – long hours, low pay, and I never could seem to do anything right. But as I worked, I found that I loved photography.

After one more apprenticeship, I went out on my own. I started by letting people know I'd shoot anything – weddings, parties, any low-paying job that no one else would take. Through people I'd met before, I got some small jobs at the Met. This included photographs for the annual Christmas catalogue. Also, my work with Lee Bolton got me jobs doing other fine art catalogues. Now I've done over 30 art books.

HOW I FEEL ABOUT IT:
I love photography; otherwise, I'd never be able to do it. The job is physically grueling. The deadlines are tight. Hours are long so it's tough to get a social life going. And running your own studio is insecure in that you're always looking for work. So if I didn't love photography, it wouldn't make sense to put up with this.

Most of the work I do in the studio is still-life shots of objects, but my favorite work is with people. In fact, the photos I'm proudest of are images from which I can't even make a living – black-and-white street scenes that I've shot in Russia, Ireland, and all over Europe. I love being in the street with a camera, and using it to see and discover.

WHAT YOU SHOULD KNOW:
Some people want to get into this field because they think it's glamorous. Others want

to get into it for money. But really, there's only one reason to do it — because you want to take pictures. If you don't have that need, and you don't love photography, you'll never be able to work hard enough to make it.

The best way to start is by apprenticing yourself to a few different photographers, so you can pick up different styles and perspectives. Also, take some workshops. But as far as photography schools go, I'm not too enthusiastic. Most of them just make you into a technician. You would do better to study humanities. Then you can bring some intelligence to your work.

The most important traits to have are tenacity and persistence. I went into photography not caring whether or not I succeeded. I only knew that it was what I wanted to do. That's how you have to approach it. Eventually, once you're established, you can make some money. But it's so hard at first that if high pay is all you're after, you'll never stick with it.

Schecter spends most of his time in the studio.

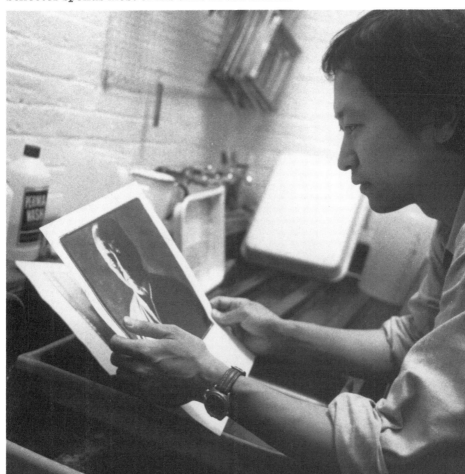

"You need to be able to visualize how things will look."

WYNN HEROU GUBRUD

FOOD STYLIST

Fridley, Minnesota

WHAT I DO:
I prepare and arrange food to be photographed and filmed. Sometimes I'm hired directly by food companies, newspapers, and magazines. Other times my work comes from agencies, photographers, and art directors who are working for these types of clients.

Food photos are used in various ways. When the photos are commissioned by food companies, they usually appear on packages, in sales brochures, and in promotional materials. Photos for newspapers and magazines are used to illustrate food-related articles, such as features about restaurants. Sometimes the food I arrange is photographed for advertisements and cookbooks.

Most jobs begin with a pre-production meeting that

includes everyone involved with the project – the stylist, the art director, the photographer, and the marketing person. If the shoot is for a television commercial, then there's a director present instead of a photographer.

At the pre-pro meeting everyone's ideas are discussed and a time for the shoot is set. For still photography, the art director's idea is shown in a drawing. If you're doing a television commercial, it's shown as a series of drawings called a storyboard. After the meeting you do the necessary planning. This includes making a list of groceries and kitchen equipment needed for the shoot.

For most shoots you prepare the food yourself. Then you arrange it at least twice. The first arrangement is a stand-in. The photographer and the art director

Wynn prepares pancakes for a photographic shoot.

Wynn personally selects the food for the shoot.

studies, I became aware of food styling. Although there were no classes in it, I read a lot about it and incorporated food styling into my projects.

After college, I spent five years doing food styling for General Mills. Then I left to have a family. Six years later I decided to get back into the business as a freelancer. From my work at General Mills I had contacts and also a strong portfolio, which I showed to agencies and photographers. Soon I began to get calls.

HOW I FEEL ABOUT IT:

There's a lot to like about this work. I have the opportunity to be creative and see immediate results from my work. I also get to work with a team of creative people — art directors, photographers, writers, and marketing people — who are all trying their hardest to do something perfectly. Also, the people on the team bring their own unique skills and perspectives. This helps me keep my own eye fresh.

I like freelancing, but it's not for everybody. I wanted flexible hours so that I could be with my sons, but there are trade-offs. Freelancers, because they work for themselves, don't receive the benefits or the security that a large company can provide.

use it to set up the lighting, the background, the props, and the positioning. By the time all that's done, though, the food usually looks pretty bad. So when they're ready to shoot, you bring in the second arrangement of food, which always looks fresh.

HOW I GOT STARTED:

My interest in food styling began when I was at the University of Minnesota. I had a major in home economics and a minor in journalism and advertising. Through my advertising

WHAT YOU SHOULD KNOW:
To get a job as a stylist with a large food company, you have to have a degree in home economics. It's a credential that shows people you have the necessary background to do the job. Photo and film shoots are costly — thousands of dollars a day — and a home-economics degree assures people that you're not an unreasonable risk.

You also need to know certain basic design prin-ciples: color, texture, size relationships, and position-ing of shapes in relation to each other. And you need to be able to visualize how things will look.

A good thing to do while getting your degree is assist in a photography studio, or intern with a food stylist. Offer your services for a certain number of weeks, even if there's no pay involved. The experience is invaluable and will help you get a job.

Wynn works closely with photographers on the set.

"Just be willing to keep yourself open and excited, because the trip is unbelievable."

B.J. GILLIAN

MAKE-UP ARTIST

New York, New York

WHAT I DO:

I'm hired to make up models for print ads and television commercials. I create a look on the face of the model, and that look helps sell the product.

My job is very much like a model's. I have an agent, and he keeps a portfolio, or book, of my work. When a client thinks that he might want to hire me, he asks to see my book. If he likes it, then I get the booking – the job. The booking is usually for a day, but it could also be a trip, or even a long-term contract for a series of ads.

For a typical job, the client shows me a sketch, a layout, or a group of photos to give me an idea of the type of ad he wants. He describes to me the model, the attitude, and the look, and then I figure out a way to achieve

B.J. touches up a model's make-up during a shoot.

that look. Once I have done this, the hairdresser and I prepare the model for photography. This takes about an hour and a half. And that's it. Usually there are very few changes, but I have had days on which I've been asked to make as many as 30 make-up changes.

HOW I GOT STARTED:

I began as a model, and I modeled my way through high school and college. But I'm only 5'8", and that's very short for modeling, so I didn't think I could keep modeling for very long. I wanted to stay in the industry because it paid so well, so I decided to look for something else in the industry that would suit me.

When you're modeling, you spend 95 percent of your time in the dressing room. Some people spend that time on homework or pursuing a hobby. But I used it to watch

31

Clients describe to B.J. the look that they want.

make-up artists. I found that working with make-up came naturally to me, so I decided to make a career of it.

There's a standard path for make-up artists who work in print ads, rather than TV or movies. My career followed that path. First you do tests. In a test, a new model, a new photographer, a new make-up artist, and a new hairdresser all get together to do a series of pictures. Because you're all inexperienced, it takes about a year to put together enough good tests for a portfolio. Then you go to Europe to really show your artistic flair, because that's where magazines are willing to take a chance hiring new talent.

HOW I FEEL ABOUT IT:
This work has been wonderful. Those years in Europe were an education. I

learned other languages, saw other countries, and was exposed to different cultures. I grew up.

The job is freelance, which has both its good and its bad points. The advantages include being able to take long periods of time off, and waking up each morning knowing that you're going to do something new. The disadvantages are that there's no stability or job security. If you don't get called one day, you begin to wonder if you'll ever get called again.

WHAT YOU SHOULD KNOW: Learning the skills is a problem. Europe has make-up schools, but in this country it's impossible to find a reputable school. Don't be taken in by ads or people who tell you anything else. The only way to pick up the skills in America is to teach yourself or learn them from watching others.

The best way to get into the business is to go to a modeling agency and tell them you want to test. From there, just be willing to keep yourself open and excited, because the trip is unbelievable. Get yourself a job waiting tables, or some other work that will support you until you go to Europe.

Another practical consideration you should be aware of is that it's much easier to get work if you know both hair design and make-up. Also, make-up is a profession for young people. As you reach 40, it's harder to get good jobs because people are always looking for something fresh and new and vibrant. They just don't think that a middle-aged person can have new ideas. So you have to be prepared to switch careers.

The industry pays quite well, but almost all fees are negotiated on a per-job basis. That means your earnings depend on the kind and number of jobs you get.

Some days B.J. has to make up to 30 make-up changes.

"The best thing about this
job is the news itself."

RICK ALLEY

ART DIRECTOR

Memphis, Tennessee

WHAT I DO:
I'm the art director for a daily newspaper called the *Memphis Commercial Appeal*. Actually, my official job title is graphics editor, which is more descriptive of the work that I do. I have a staff of seven artists under me, and I'm responsible for assigning all the graphics — the illustrations, maps, and charts — that will be used to help explain and illustrate the news.

Some of the graphics assignments are advance requests for upcoming issues. But most of our work is done on a daily basis. Each morning I meet with the paper's editors to discuss the day's news. At these meetings the editors request graphics, and I assign the requests to the staff. As the day progresses, and more news comes over

Rick reviews some art prepared for the paper.

the wire, sometimes additional requests for graphics are made, and I assign those. There's also an afternoon meeting to check on what's been done, and to see whether anything else is needed. At some point in the afternoon I give the design desk the size of each piece, so that the pages can be laid out. Then, by 5:30, we give the designers the actual graphics, so they can be used in the next day's newspaper.

HOW I GOT STARTED:
My father and grandfather were both editorial cartoonists, so I grew up knowing the newspaper business. Of course, I said to myself, "That's not for me. I'll never do that stuff." And I guess I was right about being a cartoonist — I didn't have the strong political interest it takes to do that job. But I didn't escape the newspaper business, either. When I was

Rick meets each morning with the paper's editors.

twenty, I had a summer job here. Then one of the part-time artists quit, and they let me try his job. I've been here ever since, first as an artist and illustrator and now as graphics editor.

HOW I FEEL ABOUT IT:
I liked being an artist. But after doing it for almost 20 years, I was starting to get burned out. Although the news isn't the same every day, it's on the same subjects, and you begin to run out of fresh approaches. I was happy to move on to this job because I'm no longer constantly required to generate new angles on the same topics. Some artists don't like being supervisors, but that isn't the case with me. My years as an artist gave me a thorough knowl-

edge of what's needed, and what it's like on the other side of the fence.

Probably the best thing about this job, though, is the news itself. The news involves everything in the world. So my whole day, all of my work, keeps me on top of every-thing that's going on. Instead of taking me away from the outside world, my job puts me in touch with it.

WHAT YOU SHOULD KNOW:
Like any job, the negatives and positives are affected by the people around you. The people who are in charge set the tone for the entire paper. If an editor is serious, and has a feel for news, and is committed to it — that's great. That's the way our editor is now. But I've also worked for editors who were more

committed to their way of doing things than to having things work out. You can't be that rigid and still have a good paper.

The size and competence of your staff also affects your ability to manage your workload. I'm fortunate — I have a good staff — but I'd love to have more people. My main problem is too many graphics requests and too few artists.

This is a 40-hour-a-week job, and I'm here from 10:00 in the morning until 6:00 or 7:00 each night, five days a week. How tough those hours are depends on the number of requests there are. To handle this job, you need to be patient, you need to be flexible, and you have to have the ability to perform well under deadline pressure. The job pays adequately, but if it's money you want, my advice is to go into law.

As for getting into the business, the most important thing is having a portfolio of illustrations. Also, you should know computer graphics, because that's where things are headed. Illustrations are still done by hand. But everything else — charts, maps, and other graphics — is now being done straight on the computer.

Rick's job involves supervising others.

"Dickie will never amount to anything if he keeps drawing cartoons."

DICK WRIGHT

EDITORIAL CARTOONIST

Gainesville, Virginia

WHAT I DO:
I draw cartoons about national and international political issues. I'm on the staff of the *Providence Journal-Bulletin*. My cartoons are also syndicated, which means that other newspapers buy the right to reprint them. Right now my cartoons are printed in about 190 papers nationwide.

There have been times when I have drawn cartoons five or seven days a week, but the agreement I have now calls for only four cartoons each week. On a typical morning, I have to have rough sketches of a few ideas ready by 9:30. I fax them from my home in Virginia up to my editor in Providence, Rhode Island. Then he gives me a call and we discuss which idea we're going to use. After that I sit down and

Dick works at his desk on the next day's cartoon.

draw the cartoon, which usually takes me about four or five hours. The finished cartoon is picked up by Federal Express. Then I sit down with some newspapers, or in front of the TV, and catch up on what's happening so the whole process can start all over again.

HOW I GOT STARTED:
Drawing was something that came naturally to me. Unfortunately, it wasn't always looked on as a talent. On my sixth-grade report card, my teacher wrote to my mother, "Dickie will never amount to anything if he keeps drawing cartoons." Despite that, I did keep drawing. I drew all the way up the line though grade school, high school, and college. I drew for every publication that was put out at each school.

Although I took some art courses, I developed most of

my skills by studying other artists' work. When I imitated the work of artists I admired — Walt Disney, for example, and Mort Drucker, who drew for *Mad Magazine* — I learned something. Imitating is something that young artists have to do. It teaches you how to draw. Ultimately, if you continue, you will develop your own style.

My first paying newspaper work was in 1972, when I created a comic strip that was syndicated by the *Los Angeles Times.* It was called "Party Politics," and it was about the politics of the time. Next, I was hired by the *San Diego Union* as a backup editorial cartoonist. I drew cartoons every day, but they were only used once or twice each week. Then, after a year, I was made head cartoonist. Although it was a good opportunity, it had one big drawback — lack of freedom. Topics and positions were dictated to me. Fortunately, that was the last job I've had in which conditions were so rigid.

HOW I FEEL ABOUT IT:
I feel very lucky to be doing what I'm doing. I like drawing, and it's great to be able to express your opinions. When I get done each day, I have a drawing that tells people what my opinion is. That's probably what I enjoy most about my work.

Dick puts the finishing touches on a cartoon.

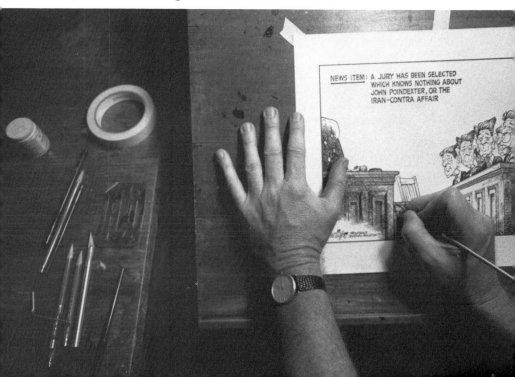

The two biggest problems I face are analyzing issues and generating ideas. There are lots of issues to choose from, but you need to understand them thoroughly in order to analyze them effectively. Also, you have to think up fresh, punchy ideas that will communicate your opinions.

WHAT YOU SHOULD KNOW: Drawing skills are only the beginning. You also need to have genuine political interest. You must have convictions or your work won't be very good. Strong analytical skills, opinions, and a consistent philosophy — that's the common thread binding almost all successful cartoonists.

There are many ways to break into the field. Some people are doing something else for a newspaper, like sportswriting, when they find out they can draw. But the best way is to start with a school newspaper. Develop a style and a philosophy. Put a portfolio together. Then, when you're out of school, go to a small newspaper and try to get your work published. Eventually, if you stick with it, you may land a regular slot.

There's a wide range of pay in the field. A staff cartoonist on a smaller regional or local newspaper may make $25,000 a year. A

Dick faxes ideas for the day's cartoon from his home in Virginia to his editor in Providence.

syndicated cartoonist, carried in 300 to 500 newspapers, can make as much as $250,000 a year. Of course, only a handful of cartoonists do that well.

"People want their houses to
reflect their personalities."

KARLA TRINCANELLO

INTERIOR DESIGNER

Hanover Township, New Jersey

WHAT I DO:

My partner and I run a full-service interior design studio, which means that space planning, or designing the look and shape of a space, is only part of what we do. After we've developed an initial design plan, we see that plan through to completion. We follow through on every detail, until we've achieved the client's desired effect.

About 70 percent of our work is with homes. First we go to the client's home and acquaint ourselves with the client's likes, dislikes, and needs. We measure and photograph each room. We also photograph any special objects or furnishings that the client wants to keep. Then, back at the studio, we come up with a plan, taking into account the budget we've

Karla looks over fabric samples for a new design.

been given. Our plan includes furniture, fabrics, wall coverings, and floor finishes, as well as suggestions for art work. After we've presented the plan, the client reacts to it and revisions are made. Then the plan is approved and the next phase of the work begins, the construction.

Because we're a full-service studio, clients can also hire us to supervise the execution of the plan. If they do, we take care of everything. We supervise and work with the architects, carpenters, electricians, carpet installers — everyone who's necessary to do the job. But clients can also hire us for the plan only, and then use their own people to do the construction work.

In addition to homes, we work with offices and restaurants. In some ways, offices are like people's homes. People want them to reflect their personalities.

But office clients also want to project a corporate image and impress people. Restaurants are different. There, the main job is to carry out a theme. We may have to create a space that has a jungle theme, or one that looks like an old antique store or a ship's dining room.

HOW I GOT STARTED:
I've always been interested in my surroundings. As a child, when I was in a house, I was always imagining a different way to arrange it. Naturally, I had dollhouses, and I rearranged them constantly.

I didn't go into this work immediately. When I first went to college, I studied business and took a job that was unrelated to interior design. But after I was married, I became involved in the design of my own home. That really sparked my interest in the field, so I went back to school and studied design. I was also working. I took a part-time job with a designer, and I learned the business from the ground up.

HOW I FEEL ABOUT IT:
The job has many rewards. I like being creative, and helping people express themselves through their environment. It's satisfying to see the finished rooms and, of course, I also love the compliments that come with them.

Client contact, too, can be rewarding. The relationship between a designer and a client is very special. It usually lasts for many years, because most people don't redo their homes all at once.

WHAT YOU SHOULD KNOW:
Many students who come to work for us have the misconception that designers have

Before beginning a plan, Karla measures each room.

Karla often works with construction tradespeople.

total control. They think, "Well, we're the designers, and the client should listen to us and follow our design." But it doesn't work that way. We try never to impose a style on our clients. Instead, we try to help them visualize their space, and we give them suggestions. But, in the end, the clients are the ones who will have to live in the space. So they should make the final decisions.

Students also underestimate the level of work and responsibility that's involved. Before they can design, they really need to see how the business works. They should work as apprentices and learn everything they can about the business. They should study the interaction between designers, clients, architects, and contractors, and see how successful projects are done.

Designers' incomes span a wide range. Most people starting out don't have many clients, so they don't make too much money. But an established designer working for wealthy clients or large companies can do extremely well, well into six figures.

"You've got to be willing to live and breathe fashion."

JOHN KARL

FASHION DESIGNER

New York, New York

WHAT I DO:

I'm a design director for a clothing manufacturer. I have my own line, or collection, of clothes – Studio H by John Karl. I'm responsible for everything about that line, right down to choosing its name and designing the label. I design the clothes, I deal with the factories, and I talk to buyers and the press.

Every clothing line begins with a concept. The Studio H concept is casual men's clothing that can be worn in a variety of different settings. These are good-looking clothes that you might use as pajamas, or for lounging around at home on the weekend. You can also wear them for jogging, tennis, or going to the beach – whatever you might do on a day off.

Once you have a concept for a line, then you move on

John adjusts the fit of a model's Studio H outfit.

to choosing the colors and the fabrics, which isn't as simple as it sounds. Think of all the different shades of blue or purple that you can, or all the different materials, blends, and weaves in clothing that you've seen. There's a lot to choose from.

Some of your decisions are dictated by the market, which is the group of people you think will be buying your particular line of clothes. For example, you may know that the people you're trying to reach like a certain type of shirt in a knit fabric rather than a woven fabric. But for most of the choices you have to make, you're relying on your own judgment.

After the concept comes the actual design and production of the clothes. I come up with silhouettes, or designs, which are made into samples. I oversee the making of samples, and when they're ready, I present these sam-

47

ples to the fashion press. Also, I present the line to buyers from stores. After orders are in, I deal with the factories, monitor production, and make sure that things stay on schedule.

HOW I GOT STARTED:
Years ago, I had an aunt who owned a nightclub in Baltimore. Her work clothes were a strapless gown and a fur coat. She slept all day and stayed out all night. To me, it was all very glamorous. Looking at her, I decided that I wanted to be involved in fashion — creating a look, making people look good.

All of John's clothing lines begin with a concept.

As time went on, I combined my interest in fashion with my skill at sketching, which is something I have always liked to do. I attended Maryland College of Art, where I majored in fashion design. I built up a portfolio. Then I got on a train, came to New York, and began pounding on doors. Eventually I worked my way up to the job I have now.

HOW I FEEL ABOUT IT:
It's very rewarding to be creative, and to see my ideas and designs produced. I also like it when buyers respond well to what I've done. But for me, the most rewarding thing is actually seeing someone wearing my clothes

John works with a model wearing a Studio H t-shirt.

as they walk down the street or stand in line for the bus.

The job's biggest challenge, besides having to be constantly creative, is time. I'm constantly juggling things. At any one time, I can be dealing with three different lines — one that's being produced, one that's in the sample stage, and one that's in the idea stage. It can add up to a lot of pressure.

WHAT YOU SHOULD KNOW:
Fashion isn't just a job; it's a commitment. It's 24 hours a day, seven days a week. You've got to be willing to live and breathe fashion. You have to be concerned with everything that's fashionable — clothes, plays, food, resorts. But that doesn't mean fashion is some sort of game.

I don't know why, but some designers come out of school and are surprised to find out that fashion is a very serious business. You're not just a designer, you're a business person. You've got to be on time. If you've got twenty salespeople on the road, waiting to sell, and the clothing is late, they don't eat. It's a huge responsibility.

Many designers make quite decent livings. Some fashion designers who've made the transition to celebrity status, such as Ralph Lauren, are very wealthy now. But even in the middle of the range, there's enough work to go around.

"The point is to show kids that art is a part of everyday life."

ELIZABETH BAILEY

ART TEACHER

Brunswick, Maine

WHAT I DO:
I teach art classes from kindergarten through sixth grade. I split my time between two schools, and see each class once a week for 45 minutes. In all, I work with about 400 students. But I feel I get to know them all quite well through the time I spend with them, and through their art.

The topics that I teach are tied loosely to my school district's art curriculum. A curriculum is a way of organizing the specific subjects that kids should be taught. Most of the topics are repeated from year to year, but in greater depth each time. For example, in kindergarten we work with colors and figure drawing. In the third grade, we still do these things, but we do more with them. Third graders

Elizabeth helps a student make a grass sculpture.

work with more colors, and are able to draw more complex pictures.

Although the curriculum provides a broad outline for my job, I have almost complete freedom in what I teach and the way in which I teach it. One thing that's really exciting to me is that more classroom teachers are seeing art as a way to link other subject areas. For example, a teacher might tell me that students in his class will be studying forests. Then I think, "What can we do with forests?" If my art topic is drawing, I might have kids look at and draw trees. Or I might have them make paper. The point is to show kids that art is a part of everyday life, and that everything is interrelated.

HOW I GOT STARTED:
As far back as I can remember, I've been drawing seriously. It's how I express

Elizabeth likes to help children express themselves.

December of my first year, it all began to click. What I learned in one class made sense in all my other classes. My painting, drawing, and art history classes were all pointing toward the same thing – making visual sense of the world.

After college, I went on to graduate school, and it was there that I became interested in teaching. As part of school, I had a teaching job. Until then I had been sure I'd never teach. Everyone in my family had taught or done social work, but I wouldn't. The moment I began teaching, though, it felt right.

HOW I FEEL ABOUT IT:

What really grabs me about teaching elementary-school art is that I'm catching children at the very beginning. I help shape, in a gentle way, their attitudes about art. It's my hope that I can give kids a positive start in working with art. I like to think that when they look back, their first memories of art will be good ones.

myself. I have dyslexia, which is a condition that affects the way the mind processes information. As a result, I have trouble with numbers. Also, while I learned to read at an early age, I've always had trouble spelling. So drawing was always my way of coping and getting a handle on things. It was my own world in which I could set the rules.

While art has always been important to me, I didn't realize how important it was until I was in college. In

Another important part of my job is working with other teachers, and building good relationships. A small school district like mine is a lot like a family. While you get the good aspects of family life – closeness, a knowledge of who's around you — the problems are there as well. Sometimes there are rivalries and communication problems.

WHAT YOU SHOULD KNOW:

To be a good art teacher, you need to be an artist. You don't have to be a great one, but you have to be passionate about it. If you know art only from theory, you won't be able to teach it. Training should start with art school, then you should learn teaching. But it all comes back to the same point: You should be an artist first.

You should also be aware of the developmental stages that children go through. You don't have to have formal training in psychology, but you need an instinct about it. I have an interest in how children think and grow and learn, and this contributes to what I bring to the job and the profession.

Teaching isn't a job you go into for the summers off or the money, though the money can be good. The real reason to go into teaching is that you're passionate about kids and art.

Working together, the students help each other to learn.

"I can make the space feel
like a 1920's dance hall or a
2001 space station."

KEVIN COYLE

SET DRESSER

Los Angeles, California

WHAT I DO:
I'm responsible for making the "look" of a film happen. The costume designers dress the actors, but I dress the set, which is the stage where the film is shot. Depending on the props I use and how I place them, I can make the space feel like a 1920s dance hall or a 2001 space station.

Here's an example of what I do: Let's say we're making a movie of what you're doing right now — reading a book. First, the construction people would come in and build the set, which would be your room. Then the set dresser — me — would come in and add the physical details that make people believe the set really is your room. I'd bring in the chair you're sitting in, a phone, a desk, maybe a pennant that shows which baseball team you root for —

Kevin thinks this statue might make a good prop.

everything right down to the last paper clip on your desk.

Some of the props I use on film sets are bought at places like thrift shops and antique stores. Others are rented from specialized prop houses. For example, if I were working on a movie about doctors and hospitals, I'd go to a medical prop house and rent operating tables and medical instruments.

HOW I GOT STARTED:
I've been interested in movies since I was little. My dad had a Super 8 movie camera, and by the time I was 9 or 10 I was shooting all kinds of little films. My friends and I filmed chase and adventure movies. We built models, then filmed them being blown up. Once we destroyed my sister's dollhouse.

All through high school I was in film classes and movie clubs. Then I went to Ohio State University, where I started with theater and moved into film. I learned all sorts of technical skills there. I also met people who got me my first jobs in film.

My first job was as an assistant director on the movie *16 Days of Glory*, which was about the 1984 Summer Olympics. For that movie, I took care of all the red tape – getting permits, coordinating security, and other details like that.

Although I learned a lot shooting *16 Days*, my next job was even more valuable. It was on the public TV series *West of the Imagination*. Because the crew for this show was small, I got a chance to do all kinds of different jobs: assistant cameraman, who helps focus the camera; grip, who moves the cameras and sets up the lights; and gaffer, who does the electrical work. Although you earn less on low-budget operations, they're great because the shows are usually more interesting and you get a chance to learn more.

HOW I FEEL ABOUT IT: Creating environments can be fascinating. Assembling a group of objects that a certain character would have accumulated over a lifetime takes a lot of thought and creativity. Some of the sets I've had to dress have been quite challenging. One set was an entire indoor beach.

There are problems with the job, though. The hours are long – 10 hours a day in preproduction, before the

Kevin measures a prop that may be useful.

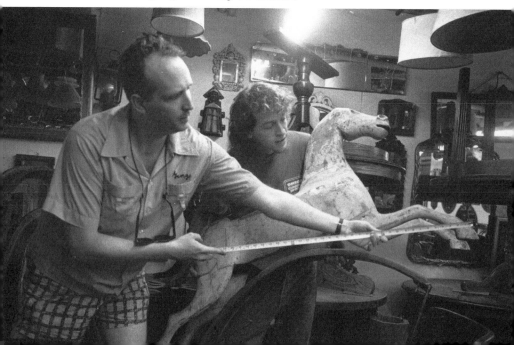

Kevin looks for items a film character might own.

movie is shot, and 12-15 hours a day during actual production. This makes it difficult to live a normal life. There's also a lot of pressure. Schedules are tight, but if a director or an art director wants things changed at the last minute to get a different look, you've got to do it. You can't complain about the changes, or ask for more time.

WHAT YOU SHOULD KNOW:
To succeed in this job, and most movie jobs, you have to be flexible and willing to work hard. You need to be able to get along with people. Everyone's under a lot of pressure, and you won't last

long if you can't control your temper.

The best way to get into the field is to come to Los Angeles and meet people. Talk to art decorators. Talk to set decorators. Contact as many people as you can, and ask them for work.

This job is different things to different people. The weekly pay ranges from $800 on smaller films to $1,200 on studio films. Some people do it as a career. Others move on to other jobs like art director, coordinating the entire look of a film and not just the sets or costumes. Eventually, I want to write and direct movies.

"Books that are created by artists can sometimes be strange."

CHRISTINA LESHOCK

ART LIBRARIAN

Philadelphia, Pennsylvania

WHAT I DO:

I'm an art librarian at the Moore College of Art and Design. My specific title is cataloguer. I decide how to organize our collection so that people who come to use the library can find things easily. For the books, this means assigning each new book a call number, and placing it under as many as 10 different subject headings in the card catalogue.

But as an art librarian, I have to catalogue a lot of things that aren't books. For example, there's a picture file in which we catalogue and describe all the paintings in our collection. And many of our "books" are not really conventional books at all.

Books that are created by artists can sometimes be strange. They may not have words, or even take the usual

Christina's specialty is classifying art books.

shape of a book. They may have nothing but artwork in them, or you might open one of these books to find that it has a hole cut out of it and a ball suspended in the middle. Whatever it is, though, I've got to find a way to catalogue it. That requires a knowledge of art.

HOW I GOT STARTED:

The arts have always been a strong interest of mine. After college I worked at a series of jobs connected to the arts. For a while I worked for a classical-music management company, and also for an alternative art magazine. These jobs kept me in touch with the arts and artists, but eventually I began searching for something better to do. I had a friend who worked in a library, and she was really enthusiastic about it. I thought that an art library might tie all my interests together. So I got a master's degree in library science, doing as many projects as I could on art-related topics. That way, when I interviewed for jobs, I could show people that I had a good background in art.

HOW I FEEL ABOUT IT:
My favorite part of this job is the material I'm working with — art, art books, art issues. Also, many of the people who work at the school are artists, and it's been enriching to work with them.

One of the biggest challenges of this job is working with the students. Art students can be very temperamental and resistant to being "library literate." They want to use the library, but only if they can understand it immediately. Despite my work, the catalogue sometimes seems like Greek to them. They get upset and jump to the conclusion that the library doesn't have what they need. It gives me satisfaction to help them find what they're looking for.

WHAT YOU SHOULD KNOW:
I went about things backwards: I got my library degree first. Usually people get a subject degree first, and then they get a library degree, although some graduate schools combine both degrees in one program. That's because it's usually impossible to become a librarian with a subject specialty if you don't have a degree in that subject. My experience was different, but I may still go back someday for a master's degree in art history.

The pay in library jobs is fairly standard — entry-level salaries range from $18,000 to $24,000 per year — but an art librarian at a large metropolitan library can make quite a good living.

Christina organizes the library's card catalogue.

Related Careers

Here are more art-related careers you may want to explore:

APPRAISER
An appraiser determines how much a work of art is worth. Appraisers often work for auctioneers and insurance companies.

ART CONSERVATOR
An art conservator restores works of art that have been damaged, such as torn paintings or broken sculptures. Art conservators also clean old paintings.

ART HISTORIAN
Art historians are experts in the history of art. Usually, they specialize in one style or one painter. Sometimes they are hired to tell whether a painting is a fake.

ART THERAPIST
An art therapist uses art to help people work through psychological problems. Patients look at pieces of art and then discuss what those images mean to them.

BOOK DESIGNER
A book designer is responsible for the look of a book. This may include everything from choosing the type style to deciding on the illustrations to be used.

COSTUME DESIGNER
Costume designers create costumes for movies, stage productions, and television. Costume design is particularly important when the story is about another time or place.

CURATOR
A curator manages a particular collection at a museum. Curators also research and lecture on the objects in their collections.

ENGRAVER
Engravers etch metal plates that are used as printing plates. The printing plates used to make postage stamps and money are made by engravers.

EXHIBIT SPECIALIST
Exhibit specialists design exhibits for museums. They supervise the mounting of the art as well as the exhibit's lighting and color scheme.

GALLERY OWNER
Art galleries sell artists' work to the general public, earning a commission on each sale.

ILLUSTRATOR
Illustrators create the art that is included in publications such as books and magazines.

SCENIC ARTIST
Scenic artists paint the backdrops for movie sets. Sometimes directors will also have scenic artists create specific paintings to decorate the set.

TEXTILE DESIGNER
Textile designers create patterns, which are then woven into the fabrics from which clothing is made.

Organizations

Contact these organizations for information about the following careers:

ART THERAPIST
American Art Therapy Association
5 E. Lawley Street, Mundelein, IL 60060

CONSERVATOR
American Institute for Conservation of Historical and Artistic Works
3545 Williamsburg Lane, N.W., Washington, DC 20008

INTERIOR DESIGNER
American Society of Interior Designers, "Career Guides"
1430 Broadway, New York, NY 10018

ART LIBRARIAN
Art Library Society, 3900 East Timrod Street, Tucson, AZ 85711

GENERAL ART-RELATED CAREERS
Careers Press
62 Beverly Road, Box 34, Hawthorne, NJ 07502

FASHION DESIGNER
Fashion Institute of Technology Placement Office
227 West 27 Street, New York, NY 10001

GRAPHIC DESIGNER, ILLUSTRATOR, CARTOONIST
Graphic Artists Guild, 11 West 20 Street, New York, NY 10011

INTERIOR DESIGN
National Council for Interior Design Qualification
118 East 25 Street, New York, NY 10010

ART TEACHER
National Education Association Instruction and
Professional Development Department
1201 16th Street, N.W., Washington, DC 20036

PHOTOGRAPHER
Rochester Institute of Technology, School of Photography
Attention: William DuBois
1 Lomb Memorial Drive, P.O. Box 9887, Rochester, NY 14623

GRAPHIC DESIGNER, INTERIOR DESIGNER, ART DIRECTOR, PHOTOGRAPHER
School of Visual Arts Attention: Joel Garrick
209 East 23 Street, New York, NY 10010

GRAPHIC DESIGNER, ILLUSTRATOR, CARTOONIST
Society of Illustrators, 128 East 63 Street, New York, NY 10021

Books

ART CAREER GUIDE
By Donald Holden. New York: Watson-Guptile Publications, 1983.

CAREERS FOR WOMEN WITHOUT COLLEGE DEGREES
By Beatryce Nivens. New York: McGraw-Hill, 1988.

CAREERS IN FILM AND VIDEO PRODUCTION
By Michael Honwin. Boston: Focal Press, 1990.

CREATIVE CAREERS
By Gary Blake and Robert W. Bly. New York: John Wiley and Sons, 1985.

DESIGN CAREERS
By Steven Heller and Lita Tolarico. New York: Van Nostrand Reinhold Co., 1987.

FAST TRACK CAREERS
By William Lewis and Nancy Schuman. New York: John Wiley and Sons, 1987.

GETTING INTO FASHION
By Melissa Jones. New York: Ballantine, 1984.

GETTING INTO FILM
By Mel London. New York: Ballantine, 1977.

MAKING IT IN THE MEDIA PROFESSIONS
By Leonard Mogel. Chester, Ct.: Globe Pequot Press, 1987.

THE NEW YORK FINE ARTIST'S SOURCE BOOK
Division of Cultural Affairs of the City of New York. New York: Addison-Wesley, 1983.

OFF BEAT CAREERS
By Al Sacharov. Berkeley, Calif.: Ten Speed Press, 1988.

OPPORTUNITIES INDUSTRIAL DESIGN
By Arthur Pulos. Skokie, Ill.: National Textbook Co., 1978.

THE SCHOOL OF VISUAL ARTS GUIDE TO CAREERS
By Dee Ito. New York: McGraw-Hill, 1987.

Glossary Index